Wheeler's Campaign

Wheeler's

Campaign

by Daniel Schantz

Art by Ned O.

STANDARD PUBLISHING
Cincinnati, Ohio   24-02914

Wheeler's Adventures

Library of Congress Cataloging in Publication Data

Schantz, Daniel.
  Wheeler's campaign / by Daniel Schantz ; art by
Ned O.
  p. cm. — (Wheeler's adventures ; 8)
  Summary: Running for office in their respective
classes at school, two brothers agree to act as each
other's campaign manager.
  ISBN 0-87403-454-X (pbk.)
  [1. Elections—Fiction. 2. Brothers—Fiction. 3.
Schools—Fiction.] I. Ostendorf, Edward, ill. II.
Title. III. Series: Schantz, Daniel. Wheeler's adven-
tures ; 8.
PZ7.S3338Wd   1988
[Fic]—dc 19   88-9618

Cover illustration by Richard D. Wahl

to all the good teachers in the world,
who make learning a joy.
With special thanks to Bradley and
East Park schools of Moberly for letting me
observe, especially Carla Blackaby's class.

Contents

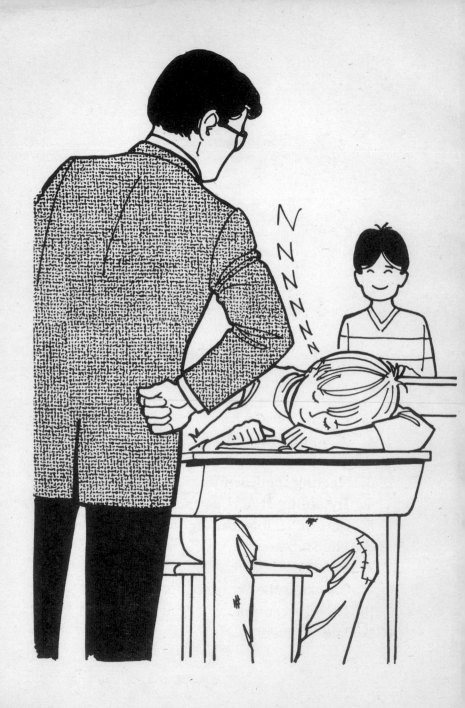

1 • Running for President

The teacher was looking right at Sonny, but Sonny was sound asleep. Mr. Watts put his chalk back in the tray and dusted his hands. Still looking at Sonny, he strolled down the aisle until he was standing right beside Sonny. A classroom full of faces turned to see what Mr. Watts would do.

Sonny's face sagged against the desk top like warm jello. Saliva drooled from his lower lip, and his right arm pillowed his head. His eyes were closed, but they twitched and jerked from a dream going on in his head.

The class was snickering now. They watched Sonny sleep on, unaware that he was being watched by the teacher. Then Mr. Watts reached out to shake Sonny and wake him, but before he could touch him, Sonny awoke with a sleep jerk and a yell. His hand smacked Mr. Watts in the face.

The class screamed with joy, and Mr. Watts smiled a patient smile. "Taking a little field trip, Sonny?" he asked.

Sonny looked around at the class with dazed eyes. A long, shiny slobber dripped down from his chin. His face was red and wrinkled, and the hair over his forehead stuck out like weeds.

Mr. Watts motioned for the class to calm down as he made his way back to the chalkboard.

"Now, as I was saying," Mr. Watts went on, "we have two nominations for President of the United States." With a strong had he wrote on the board the names "Jonah Yoder" and "Sonny Wheeler."

Sonny sat up straight and looked around. "Me?" he whispered to the blonde girl across the aisle. "Somebody nominated *me?*" He wiped a slobber from his lip.

"Yeah, *you!* I nominated you. Now cool it before you get me in trouble."

Mr. Watts drew part of a calendar on the chalk-board. Then he turned and smiled at the class.

"As I was saying, we are starting a unit on the American system of election, better known as 'politics.' In order to make this unit more interesting, we have decided to hold a presidential election. Right here in this room." He brushed chalk dust from his shirt. "Now, here is what we're going to do."

He scrawled the word "speeches" on the calendar. "On Wednesday, Sonny and Jonah will kick off the election campaign with their speeches."

Sonny's hand shot up. "You mean I have to get up front and give a speech?"

The class giggled.

"That's the idea, Sonny."

Sonny looked all around at his friends with a silly smirk. Then he raised his hand again and stood up. "But what do I talk about, Mr. Watts?"

"Oh, you can tell us about yourself and what you would like to see done. Talk about the *issue*. Remember? We decided our issue would be whether or not Mulberry should build a new school. You said you were in favor of a new one."

"Oh, yeah," Sonny muttered to himself. "I forgot."

Again the class giggled, and Sonny seemed to enjoy it.

Jonah Yoder, the Amish boy, jumped up. "Well, I think it's stupid to build a new school." He played with his suspenders, stretching them out and letting them snap back with a "smack."

Some of Jonah's friends cheered for him.

Mr. Watts waved his hands for order. "Wait a minute, wait a minute. You're getting ahead of me. Now just sit down, both of you, and relax."

The boys glared at each other and sat back down.

Mr. Watts gripped a fresh piece of chalk and glanced at the calendar. "You boys will both have a chance to state your ideas. As I was saying, you will give your speeches on Wednesday, November the second. That's the day after tomorrow." Next, he wrote the word "debate" on the chalkboard calendar. "Then on Thursday, the two of you will debate the issue. You can argue to your hearts' content for a solid hour each, if you like."

Sonny grinned big and threw a victory sign at Jonah. Jonah frowned back.

Mr. Watts rolled up his sleeves, and looked pleased with himself. "Now, the fun part," he said. "On Monday, the seventh, we are going to push back the chairs and have a political convention, right here in this room."

The kids looked around at each other with puzzled brows.

"You can make banners," Mr. Watts added. "I'll bring balloons and refreshments . . . and I'll see if we can't get some music in here. We'll have ourselves a good time."

Now the class glowed. Some of them let out a series of cheers.

A hand shot up. "When *is* the election?" a small voice asked.

Mr. Watts drew a bold star on the calendar. "Tuesday, November the eighth. The day after the convention. Elections are always held the first Tuesday after the first Monday in November." He put down the chalk and looked around the room, thinking. "Now, which one of you two candidates wants to be the Republican?"

"I wanna be the Democrack," Jonah shouted.

"Democrack? You mean the *Democrat.*"

"Yeah, that's what I mean. The Democrat."

"Is that okay with you, Sonny?"

"Sure, I wanted to be the publican anyhow."

"*Republican,* not publican, Sonny. A publican is a tax collector."

"Yeah, the *Republican*—that's me." He said it over and over to himself, softly. The class murmured with laughter.

The bell for recess rang and the kids began to clear their desks. Mr. Watts shouted above the noise, "Remember, get behind your candidate. Talk him up if you want him to win."

The girls walked out the door in a neat row, and the boys pushed and shoved behind them.

When Sonny reached the paved playground, Jonah Yoder came bouncing up to him on a pogo ball.

"Hey, Wheeler!"

"*Mr. President* to you, Odor," Sonny fired back. "You might as well get used to the sound of it." Sonny strutted around with a softball bat, waving it like a scepter.

Jonah sneered. "Ain't nobody gonna vote for somebody who sleeps in class," he warned.

Sonny just smiled back. "Ain't nobody gonna vote for nobody who ain't got no good grammar," he teased.

"Ya? Well, I'll tell you something, Wheeler. I'm so sure I'm gonna win, I ain't even gonna advertise or nothin'."

Sonny swung the bat around, trying to think of

something to say. "Okay by me," he said, finally. "Just makes my job easier. Besides, you don't need to advertise. They can *smell* you a hundred yards away."

Jonah played with his suspenders smartly. "Yep, I can see it now," he went on, ignoring Sonny's words. "Sonny Wheeler shinin' my shoes, totin' my books . . ."

"What are you talkin' about?" Sonny asked. "If you were king of the world I wouldn't carry your books."

Jonah looked at Sonny intently. "You mean you slept through that part too?"

"What part?" Sonny wanted to know.

"The part about the winner! Mr. Watts said whoever wins the election gets to be waited on by everybody else for a whole day."

Sonny raised an eyebrow. "What? You mean I get a room full of free slaves?"

"*I* get the slaves. And *you* will be one of them," Jonah fired back. He bounced away on the pogo ball, waving his black, wide-brimmed hat like a rodeo rider. "Yahoo!" he yelled.

Some of the kids swarmed around Sonny. "We're going to vote for you, Sonny," one of them said.

"Yeah," another boy added, "If you win, maybe we'll get a new school."

Sonny puffed up to his full height. "Okay, I'll give it my best shot. If you got any good ideas, let me know, okay?"

The rest of recess, Sonny walked around shaking hands and getting promises of votes.

2 • The New Deal

Before the last bell of the day stopped ringing, Sonny was racing down the hallway for home. He slid down the ramp to the lower level, then crashed his body into the door.

As he flew across the schoolyard, he could see his parents in the distance, busy raking leaves. Out of one eye he could see his brother Earnest racing to catch up with him.

Both boys leaped the fence at the same time, fell down, staggered up, ran to the yard, and dropped into the same big pile of freshly-raked leaves.

Mr. Wheeler smiled at the pile of leaves with laughs leaking out of it. "Pull up a rake," he said, when their heads popped out of the pile.

Sonny jumped up and brushed himself off. "Presidents don't do leaves," he said firmly.

"Presidents?" his mother asked, putting on her garden gloves.

Sonny nodded. "Yep. You are looking at the next President of the United States."

Earnest jumped up. "Yo! You too? Is the sixth grade having elections too?"

"Yeah," Sonny replied with a touch of disappointment. "Don't tell me you got nominated too, Earnest."

Earnest smiled and nodded. "Who are you running against?"

"*Odor,* " Sonny said, with a chuckle. "Can you believe it? I get *Odor* for an opponent?"

"You mean Jonah Yoder, the Amish kid?"

"That's the one."

Mrs. Wheeler raised an eyebrow. "Odor? How come you call him that?"

Sonny and Earnest smiled at each other. "'Cause he stinks," they said in unison.

"Stinks? You mean he's dirty?"

"Naw, not really," Sonny explained. "He does

the milking before he comes to school, and you can smell barnyard wherever he goes. It's on his boots."

Mr. Wheeler scratched his head. "I didn't know Amish people got into politics."

"You don't know Odor," Sonny replied. "Odor is a *rebel*. He's different from what you expect, you know? Like, you should see him. He comes to school on roller skates. He has a little TV in his lunch box . . . and always a paperback sticking out of his back pocket. He wants to be President of the United States. I mean, for *real*."

Mrs. Wheeler shook her head. "Sounds like a very interesting boy, but I don't think you should call him 'Odor.'"

"Oh, it's okay. He calls himself that. He's real nice, actually. And, hey, can he ever hit a softball. Whoom! It's outta the park!"

Sonny turned to Earnest. "Who you running against?"

Earnest cringed. "You really need to know?"

"Don't tell me it's that Evans kid?"

"*Worse!* Try Shirley Bratley."

"Sugar Brat?"

"That's the one. She's a Democrat. I'm a Republican."

Mrs. Wheeler handed her rake to Earnest. "Sugar Brat? Where did she get a nickname like that, for Heaven's sake?"

"It's her personality," Earnest explained. "She's a real brat, but she tries to cover it up by acting sweet. Believe me, it doesn't work."

Sonny nodded. "I've heard. She dresses like someone twenty-one years old."

Mrs. Wheeler threw up her hands. "I don't know why we go to the trouble of picking nice names for our children when they never use them."

"Well," Earnest fired back, "you guys do the same thing."

"Oh?"

"Sure. You call Dad 'Grease Monkey,' and he calls you 'Buttercup.'"

Mrs. Wheeler laughed. "I guess you're right. I forgot about that."

For a while the four of them busily raked leaves. Sonny held the plastic trash bags and Earnest swept the spicy-smelling leaves into the green sacks.

Sonny grew tired, so he sat on the grass to think. At last he said, "Somehow I can't picture you as a president, Earnest. I mean, presidents are supposed to be tall and good-looking, like me."

Earnest kept on raking, ignoring his brother's bragging.

Sonny kept still, knowing Earnest would say something sooner or later. And in a couple minutes Earnest stopped and glared at Sonny.

"If you ever become president, Sonny, you'll get the prize as the worst-dressed president in American history."

"Oh, is that so? Well, let me tell you something—"

Mr. Wheeler swung his rake between the two of them. "Wait a minute. Wait just a big minute," he growled. "Do I hear another contest shaping up here?"

The boys hung their heads guiltily.

"Just once, why don't the two of you *help* each other instead of *fighting* each other?"

"Right," Mrs. Wheeler joined in. "It seems to me you both would have a better chance of winning if you acted as each other's agents instead of fighting each other."

Earnest looked puzzled. "What do you mean?"

"Just what I said. You promote *Sonny*, and Sonny promotes *you*."

The boys made faces at each other.

"*Me?* Promote *him?* " Sonny said. "What's to promote?"

Well, you might be surprised at the good things you find in your brother if you really look for them."

Sonny peered into Earnest ear. "Nothing here," he quipped.

"Seems to me," his mother went on, "that if you both go around bragging on yourselves, you'll come across really stuck up. Not good if you want to win an election."

Earnest was deep in thought. "It might work," he said under his breath. He glanced at his brother. "But it won't be easy."

Mr. Wheeler studied his watch a moment. "I've got to get back to the shop. That oil should be drained out by now."

"And I've got to get supper on," Mrs. Wheeler added. "You boys finish up these leaves, please."

"I have a better idea," Sonny snapped. "Let's just cut down all these trees and we won't have to do this every year."

His parents gone, Earnest scratched his chin and said, "You know, maybe Mom and Dad are right. Let's try it. I'll promote you, and you promote me."

Sonny curled his lower lip and wrinkled his brow. "Yeah, but how do I know you'll promote *me* as hard as I promote *you*?"

"Because. See, if you win your election, then I win our contest. If you lose, then I lose our contest . . . and I don't want to lose."

"It sounds awfully complicated," Sonny whined.

"No, it's simple, see? If I win, you win, and if you win, I win. If we both get elected, then we both win."

"What if we lose?" Sonny asked.

"Well, that can't happen. Look, I can beat Sugar Brat with my eyes closed. Nobody likes her anyway."

Sonny's face lit up. "Odor should be easy to beat. He's not even gonna advertise!"

A strong gust of cool October wind showered them with leaves. Another gust snatched the trash bag from Sonny's hand, filled it with air and sailed it up in the sky like a balloon.

"Hey, look at that!" The plastic bag climbed higher and higher until it was sailing over the garage. Then it collapsed and dropped into a small pine tree at the edge of the highway.

Suddenly Sonny dashed away to the garage. He

was back in a flash, with a ball of string in his hand. With his finger he punched three holes in the edge of a fresh trash bag, then tied the string through the holes and back on itself.

Soon a large gust of wind snatched the bag from his hand and pulled it up in the air. Sonny played out string until the trash kite was high above the trees. He stood there looking proud of his invention. Then he handed the string to Earnest. "Here, hold this. I gotta go to the bathroom."

He started into the house.

"Hey! Wait! What about our deal?" Earnest called after him.

Sonny stopped and thought a second. "Okay. You got it. I'm your campaign manager and you're mine." He pointed a warning finger at Earnest. "But if I lose on account of you . . ."

3 • Meeting the Enemy

After supper Earnest went to his room to organize his campaign, and Sonny skipped outside to his old car. For over an hour he decorated the old car with streamers, stickers, and signs. On the roof he fixed a sign that said,

CAMPAIGN HEADQUARTERS
Sonny Wheeler, Manager

In the windows he taped crude signs that said, "Vote for Earnest."

It was almost dark when Earnest peered out his bedroom window to see what had happened to Sonny. When he saw the car he let out a moan. "Tacky, Sonny, really tacky. I never shoulda made this deal." He began setting out dress clothes for the next day. "If I'm gonna be president," he mumbled to himself, "then I've got to look like a president."

On Tuesday morning Earnest was chomping on corn flakes when Sonny shuffled into the kitchen. He was wearing a Disneyland T-shirt with a picture of Dumbo the elephant on the front. Above the elephant he had printed, "Republican," with a purple marker. He twirled around so the family could read the back of the shirt, which said, "Earnest for President."

Earnest choked on his cereal. "Sonny," he said, "you have all the class of a bag lady."

When Earnest got to school, he went straight to Sonny's sixth grade room. Mr. Watts was putting an assignment on the chalkboard. Only three kids were in the room so far, and they were busy watching out the window.

"Mr. Watts?" Earnest asked, matter-of-factly.

Mr. Watts turned around. "Oh, hi there. Aren't you Sonny's brother?"

Earnest nodded. He handed Mr. Watts a small computer-printed poster and said, "I was wondering if I could put one of these on each desk in the room?"

Mr. Watts read the paper and smiled. "So you're stumping for your brother, huh? Nice idea."

"Stumping?"

"Uh-huh. That's what they call it in politics when you're running for office." He glanced one more time at the paper. "Sure. Go ahead and put these on the desks. Do you have an extra one for the bulletin board?"

Earnest neatly laid a poster on each desk. Soon Sonny's name stared up from every desk top in bold letters.

As he turned to leave, Jonah Yoder pranced into the room with a softball in his hand. He looked at Earnest, then at the posters.

"What's the matter?" he said. "Your big brother has to have someone to run his show for him, Wheeler?"

Earnest stiffened. "I'm doing this cause I want to."

Jonah rolled the softball smartly up his arm and juggled it to the other hand. "Well, why don'tcha do it in your own room and leave us alone?"

Earnest turned red in the face. He headed for the door, then stopped and looked back. "You know," he said in a biting tone, "This room smells funny. Kinda like . . . like *manure*."

Jonah pretended to fire the softball at Earnest, but Earnest shot through the doorway and ran for his locker.

Meanwhile, Sonny was on his way to Earnest's room to stump for him. When he got there, he paused in the doorway. Mrs. Black was standing very straight and tall on the other side of the room, by her desk. She was not smiling, but neither was she frowning, so Sonny took a deep breath and clomped inside. He was almost to the teacher when a strong whiff of perfume made him stop.

He turned around and looked for its source. There in the middle seat of the front row sat Shirley Bratley. She was wearing a smart wool jumper and matching jacket. Shafts of light flashed from the diamond earrings on her ears. She smiled an evil smile at Sonny as she played slowly with the large pearls of her necklace.

Sonny wrinkled his nose at her, and it seemed to please her. She yawned and slouched in her chair and crossed her feet as if to say, "I've got everything under control." Sonny noticed her high heels and sneered at her again.

"May I help you, young man?" The teacher was saying. Sonny whirled around. "Uh, yeah. Can I make an announcement, Mrs. Black? Just a real quick one."

The teacher nodded and held up her hand to quiet the class. "I don't like all this noise I'm hearing," she said, then added, "Sonny Wheeler has an announcement to make. Let's listen up."

The class grew quiet, looking very curious. Sonny fastened his thumbs in his front pockets and looked around happily. "I just wanna say that my brother Earnest will make a great president for you. I mean, he's real smart and everything. He could organize an army . . . with his eyes closed."

Sonny looked sheepishly at the teacher, then back at the class. "Well, I guess that's all." He shrugged a thanks, then headed for the door.

Shirley Bratley saw him coming. She pretended to ask something of the girl behind her. At the same time she slid her left foot forward into Sonny's path.

Sonny hit the floor so hard the room quivered. The class giggled. Sonny rolled over and glared at Shirley, then at the teacher. Mrs. Black was

coming at a run, but before she got to him, Shirley slid from her seat and knelt over him.

"Oh, Sonny," she sang out sweetly, "I'm sooooo sorry. Are you okay? Here, let me help you. Oh, I'm so sorry. You poor thing. I feel so bad."

"I'll bet you're sorry," Earnest growled from the doorway. He shuffled in and plopped down into his seat. Then he mumbled, "But not as sorry as you're going to be when you lose the election."

Mrs. Black checked Sonny for injuries. Then Sonny hobbled out of the room, rubbing his knees as he went.

The school day went slowly. After school, Sonny and Earnest walked together toward home.

"Are you sure it wasn't just an accident?" Sonny asked.

"Are you kidding?" Earnest fired back. "Nothing Sugar Brat does is an accident. Trust me, if her foot was in the way, it was there for reason."

Sonny nodded. "I suppose you're right. Hey, I forgot to ask you what issue your class is using for the election."

"The cafeteria, what else?"

"You really don't like that place, do you?"

"The *place* is okay. It's the *food*. And we only get fifteen minutes to eat."

"I know what you mean. I get tired of eating plants. Just once I would like to sink my pearls into a slab of pizza instead of green beans."

"Sugar Brat likes it the way it is," Earnest explained. "You know how she is, always trying to sound grown up. She always takes the teacher's side. Good nutrition and all that health stuff."

The boys tromped into the kitchen and dropped their gym bags by the door.

"Don't leave your gym bags by the door," a voice growled from the oven. Mrs. Wheeler was on her knees, cleaning it.

"By the way," the voice added, "There's a package for you, Earnest, on the dining room table. Came in the mail today."

"A package? Who from?" He stepped into the dining room and came back with a large flat package wrapped in old, wrinkled brown paper.

"Sure is heavy."

"What is it? Who's it from?" Sonny asked, sounding a bit jealous.

"I dunno." Earnest peeled a card off the package and opened it first. "It's a birthday present . . . from Grandma Wheeler."

Sonny winced. "But it isn't your birthday."

Earnest shook his head. "I know!"

Mrs. Wheeler rolled her eyes. "Poor old Grandma. She gets so mixed up sometimes. Remember when she sent you a pair of panty hose for Christmas, Sonny?" She stood up and pulled off her rubber gloves.

Mr. Wheeler ambled into the kitchen, chuckling to himself. "That's nothing. When I was in Vietnam she sent me a red wool sweater and matching scarf. Can't you just see me tramping through the jungle in that? I traded it for a bag of ice."

Earnest grinned and kept peeling the brown paper from the box. "With my luck I'll probably get a nightgown. No, it's too heavy for that. Probably a big box of silverware or dishes." The paper dropped to his lap. "It's . . . it's a box of . . . it's a box of chocolates!"

Mrs. Wheeler leaned over and sniffed the candy. "Good," she said, "I'll just take these off your hands."

Earnest pulled the box away from her. "Wait a minute," he said with a gleam in his eye. "I think maybe I can *use* these."

Before he could close the lid, his mother snatched a square one and tossed it into her mouth.

4 • Trembling Hands

Before going to bed, Earnest opened the big box of forty-eight chocolates. The room filled with a rich, cocoa aroma.

Carefully he removed one layer of chocolates and gently laid them into another chocolate box he had found in the attic. Now he had two boxes with one layer in each.

Mrs. Wheeler appeared in the doorway. "Mm-mmm, do I smell something good in here?" She was smiling a guilty smile.

Earnest pitched her a chocolate-covered cherry.

"Good night, Mom," he warned, and she disappeared up the stairs.

At midnight she came downstairs again to get an aspirin form the kitchen cabinet. She stumbled through the dark hallway to the dining room, then stopped. She stared at the door to Earnest's room. An eerie blue light and electric smell oozed through the cracked door. She peeked in.

"Earnest? What's wrong? Are you okay?"

Earnest sat hunched over his computer screen, looking miserable. "I can't sleep," he said with a sigh.

"What is it?" his mother asked, stepping inside and sitting on the bed. "What's the problem?"

Earnest fidgeted in his seat. "It's this *speech* I have to make tomorrow." He ripped a page from the printer. "I've written it seventeen times. It gets worse each time."

His mother reached for the paper and held it to her face for a few moments.

"There's not a thing wrong with this speech, Earnest. It's lovely."

Earnest hung his head, and tears welled up in his eyes. He quickly turned away from his mother. "But Mom, you don't understand." His voice was tight and strained. "I've never given a speech before in my whole life." He wiped his wet face with his palms and took a deep breath.

"Then just make it short and sweet, Earnest. Real presidents seldom speak very long. Remember the Gettysburg Address."

Earnest tooked a deep breath and let it out slowly. His whole body was trembling. "It's not just that, Mom."

"Well, what is it?"

Earnest sniffed three times and wiped his nose with his knuckles. "I'm *scared* to give a speech. What if they all laugh at me? I'll just die. I'll never live it down."

"Die? Never? Never is a long time."

"Not for weeks, at least," Earnest replied. "Well, not for a few days, anyway."

"How many days?"

"One, at least."

"So, what if they laugh at you? Will you really die from laughter?"

"I sure would."

"Oh? I don't remember anyone ever dying from laughter. I think your class could use a few good laughs. They might even like you *more* for it."

"But Mom, you don't get it, do you? I've *got* to make a good speech."

"So you can be president?"

"No, not just that."

"Then what?"

"Because. I want to go into business when I grow up, you know? If I can't make one measly little speech now, what will I do when I have to make speeches all the time?"

Mrs. Wheeler threw up her hands. "Whoa! Just a minute here. Now you're getting far out into space.

"Look, Earnest, you're only eleven. It will be at least fifteen years before you have to give speeches. Give yourself some time, for Heaven's sake." She paused and grinned. "Besides, people change their minds. By the time you are twenty-five you may decide to be a fireman or a jet pilot or a garbage collector."

"But what if my mind goes blank. I mean, pffft! Nothing! Dad says the human brain starts working the minute you are born and never stops until you stand up to give a speech."

"Your Dad is teasing you. If your mind goes blank, just read your notes and sit down." She shoved the speech outline into his hand. "Now, you take this paper and read it over twice. Ask God to help you with it. Then go to bed. In the morning, read over it twice, then get up there and just *have fun*."

Earnest nodded. A very slight grin showed on his lips.

"Thanks, Mom. I feel better now."

At breakfast Wednesday, Sonny was wiping pancake syrup from his lips when Earnest strolled into the kitchen. "Whoooo! And who is this?" he said, when he saw how Earnest was dressed. Earnest was wearing pleated gray slacks with a white shirt and gray vest. A black tiepin stuck out of his red tie, and his cuffs were held together with matching black tacks.

"Are you going to a fashion show, or what?" Sonny teased.

Earnest said nothing, not then and not during breakfast. He left without even saying good-bye. His face was pale and stern, like someone about to take his first airplane ride.

When his class started, Shirley Bratley was first to give her speech. She stood by the teacher's desk, tottering from one leg to the other and rambling on about how nice the cafeteria is. Her left hand played with her pearl necklace and her right hand clutched an index card of notes. From time to time she paused to chew her gum and look smug.

The teacher paced slowly around the room as Shirley talked. She gave a mean look to a group of boys who were whispering. "I'm having trouble hearing," she warned. One of the boys mumbled, "Get a hearing aid."

Meanwhile, Earnest was chewing the erasers off all his new pencils and spitting the rubber crumbs on the floor. When the erasers were gone, he gnawed at the wooden part until the pencils looked like they had been run over several times by an army tank. From time to time he picked up his notes and read them with moving lips.

Shirley droned on and on. The kids in the class began to yawn, and Mrs. Black kept glancing at her watch. One small boy in front began flying his math book through the air like a helicopter, landing it on his head.

Earnest was breathing hard now, like someone who had just returned from a race. His face and hands were clammy and stiff, and he swallowed over and over again. He checked his finger watch, then folded his notes and scrunched them into his shirt pocket.

At last Shirley shuffled to her seat, and several of her friends gave her a weak cheer. "Way to go, Sugar."

Earnest could feel his heart thundering in his chest and blood throbbing through his eyes and ears. He could tell his ears were hot and red.

"Okay, class," the teacher was saying. "We have just enough time for Earnest to give his speech. Better listen up if you want to get to recess on time."

Earnest swallowed once more, then wobbled to his feet. For a moment he just stood there, trying to remember how to walk. He took one step, then another. Now he began walking faster and faster. Too fast. When he got to the front of the room, he got tangled in his own feet, staggered and sprawled face first to the floor by the chalkboard.

The class giggled, but Earnest leaped up and acted as if nothing had happened.

"Quiet!" Mrs. Black warned.

Earnest turned around and faced the class. Chalk dust clung to his red tie and his hair was sticking up in back. He opened his notes.

"If I'm elected president," he began, but his voice was a mere whisper.

The teacher looked impatient. "You'll have to speak up," she yelled from the back of the room. "We can hardly hear you."

Earnest cleared his throat and began again in

the strongest voice he could find.

"IF I'M ELECTED PRESIDENT—" he boomed so loud he startled himself. He studied his notes for the next line. "If I'm elected president . . ." He stopped and turned red in the face. The notes dropped from his hands, and he began searching all his pockets for something. "I've got the wrong notes," he mumbled. The class started giggling, but Mrs. Black shushed them.

Then Earnest began again. "If I'm elected president . . ."

"You said that *four times*," Shirley Bratley whined. She rolled her eyes.

Suddenly Earnest looked angry. He glared at Shirley and blurted out, "If I'm elected president I will make sure certain types of people are not allowed in the cafeteria."

Some of Earnest's friends cheered him. Now he began to talk rapidly and easily, hardly even looking at his notes. He spoke of his plans to lengthen the lunch hour, then drew a diagram on the chalkboard to show how he would rearrange the tables for more space. The class listened well, their eyes locked on Earnest.

And suddenly it was over. There was a ripple of applause as he took his seat. The bell rang just as he sat down, but he never joined the others in the rush to recess.

Soon he was the only one left in the room, except for Mrs. Black. She strolled over to him and knelt beside his desk. Earnest was staring straight ahead as if in a trance.

She looked into his face, and her eyes glowed. "Are you sure that's the first speech you've ever given?"

Earnest nodded weakly.

Mrs. Black stood up. "Well, Earnest, I don't mind telling you that was a truly *wonderful* speech. In fact, I know adults who can't speak that well."

Earnest mumbled a thank-you as she walked away. Then he glanced up to the ceiling and mumbled another thanks to Heaven. Finally, he put his head down on his desk and fell sound asleep.

5 • Getting It Together

When school let out Wednesday, Earnest walked downtown to the library instead of going straight home. He came out a few minutes later with an armload of books about food and vitamins.

He was almost home when Cherry, the neighbor girl, joined him. She was wearing a leaf-print blouse with a wool skirt the same rusty shade as her hair. She tromped beside him in her boots, trying to read the titles of his books.

"Whatcha doin' with all the books on vitamins?" she asked sweetly. "You on a diet or something?"

Earnest shook his head. "Nope, I'm running for president, and I need these books to get ready for my debate." He stopped and looked intently at Cherry. "Listen, this is where *you* come in. I need your help if I'm gonna win."

Cherry shrugged. "What can I do?"

"I'll show you," Earnest promised. "C'mon."

The two of them traipsed up the driveway and into the house. Earnest hung up his vest and tie, then reached into the closet for the chocolates. He set them down on the bed and opened the box.

Cherry's face began to glow. "*Chocolates!*" she squealed. "Oh, I LOVE chocolates!"

Earnest grinned an evil grin. "I know, I know," he muttered.

"Oh, can I have some, Earnest, please? Oh, pretty pretty pretty please?"

Earnest picked out a chocolate with a curl on top. He held it to her lips, then pulled it away, teasing her.

"I'll tell you what I'm gonna do, Cherry. I'm gonna *give* you these chocolates." He smiled a clever smile. "For helping me."

Cherry reached for the box, but Earnest

snatched it away. "I'll do anything, Earnest," she said in a desperate, whispery voice.

"I thought so," Earnest said under his breath. He stuffed a chocolate-covered cherry in her mouth, and she chewed it greedily, till brown juice dribbled down her chin.

"That's a down payment," he said. He looked all around, then lowered his voice to a whisper. "Now, here's the deal. I need information . . . and I need *dis*-information, understand?"

Cherry shook her head and licked her thumb. Her eyes were wide and innocent.

Earnest groaned. "What do I have to do, draw you a *picture?* Look, I want you to spy—er, I mean, nose around and find out what Sugar Brat is up to. Do you know who I mean?"

Cherry nodded. "The girl who wears heels to school?"

Earnest stuffed another chocolate in her mouth. "And anytime you get a chance, I want you to say something bad—er, I mean *negative* about her. You know, like, 'Sugar Brat is a real dummy, and I would never vote for her in a million years.'"

Cherry backed away. "I . . . I don't know about that part. That doesn't sound like a very nice thing to do."

Earnest wrinkled his brow. "Relax, Cherry. This is the way it's done. All the time."

Cherry stared sadly at the floor.

Earnest plucked another chocolate from the box and waved it slowly under her nose. "I'll trade you chocolates for secrets."

"Well," she said softly, "I guess so." She grabbed the chocolate and popped it into her mouth.

While Cherry and Earnest were talking, Sonny was outside in his old car, just talking to himself out loud. "Gotta do something big. Real big. Something that will pop their eyes, but what? There's gotta be a way."

He crawled out of his car, stretched and started away to do his chores. A sound in the sky caused him to look up, toward the sun. he saw a small airplane buzzing back and forth, high in the sky. Behind it trailed a bright, billowy plume of smoke.

"Well, I'll be . . ." The plane's smoke was carefully, slowly spelling out the name of a popular soft drink.

"Now, that's what I call BIG. If only I had an airplane." He watched until the plane flew away to the south, then sadly, slowly moseyed out to the used car lot to do his chores.

He cleaned the windshields on the cars, then checked each car for damages or theft. All the while he kept glancing at the sky to watch the big letters dissolving in the wind.

Finally he was done except for picking up trash that had blown on to the lot. He found a big plastic lard bucket and began walking the rows of cars, dropping cans and paper into it. He was almost done when he came across the green trash bag that had blown away when he was raking leaves. He started to stuff it into the bucket, then stopped. He looked up at the sky, then down at the trash bag.

Suddenly he dropped the bucket and dashed away to the garage. For a few moments he stood in the doorway, looking around and thinking. Then he grabbed a ladder and opened it up by the rafters and scampered up it. For some time he wrestled with old boards, window screens, and a heavy old roll of carpeting. Then his eyes lit up.

"Ah-hah! I knew they were here somewhere." He reached for two long cane fishing poles that were buried under the carpeting.

By the time he wrestled them out and down to the ground, he was covered with dust and carpet fibers, mixed with sweat.

He dragged the ungainly poles outside and laid them on the grass. With a strong jerk he tore the old rotten fishing line from each pole. "Wow, these must be fifteen feet long. These will be perfect."

He turned one pole sideways, forming a large

cross on the ground. Then he stepped back to admire his idea.

"Yep, this will do it. Look out world, here comes Sonny Wheeler."

At supper time Earnest was reading a book at the table when the rest of the family arrived. He sipped his milk and said, "Did you know that strawberries have more iron and vitamin C than spinach?"

His mother set a platter of potato-chip-baked chicken on the table, then snatched the book form his hands. "That's nice," she growled, "and did you know that people who read at the table get spinach shortcake for dessert?"

Mr. Wheeler prayed a long prayer for the food. Sonny kept pinching bits of potato chips from his chicken and sucking them during the prayer, until his mother kicked his shins under the table. After the prayer he looked at his mother and said, "Mom, do you have any old bed sheets I can have?"

"Bed sheets? Oh, I 'spect. Somewhere. What on earth for?"

"Just a project I'm working on. Can't tell. It's something to help my little brother get elected president of the fifth grade."

Mrs. Wheeler smiled. "Then you took our idea after all, didn't you? You're going to campaign *for* each other?"

"Well, yes," Sonny admitted.

Earnest looked puzzled. "How are old bed sheets gonna help me win the election? What are you gonna do, tie up Sugar Brat for me?"

"You'll see, soon enough. Pass the corn, please." Sonny piled a little mountain of corn on his plate, drenched it in butter, and added, "By the way, what are *you* doing to promote *me*, Earnest?"

Earnest smiled a smug smile. "It's a secret for now. But I've at least got the girls' votes guaranteed."

Mrs. Wheeler looked at her sons with pride. "Earnest, how did that speech go that you were so worried about?"

Earnest glanced at his brother. "Worried? Who, me? It was okay. No big deal."

"And Sonny? How did yours turn out?"

"No sweat," he replied calmly. "Speeches are easy for me. I just winged it. I opened my mouth and the words just flowed out. Practically got a standing ovation."

Earnest wrinkled his nose. "Oh, brother."

6 • The Debates

Shirley Bratley was the first one to give her side of the debate on Thursday. The teacher put two music stands in front of the room for podiums, one for Earnest and one for Shirley.

"Let's begin with Shirley," the teacher said, but Shirley was already out of her seat. She clicked her high heels all the way to the stand. her friends cheered for her. "Go, Sugar! You can do it."

Shirley looked pleased with herself. Her blonde bangs curled up smartly from her forehead. She smiled and smacked her gum at the same time.

With both hands she held her note card to her face, as if to show off the two oversized rings she was wearing on each hand.

The class became very quiet. Shirley cleared her throat and began speaking with a silky-sweet voice.

"Okay ... like, I wanna say, like, I'm happy with the cafeteria the way it is, you know? And, uh, like I think the cooks are really great and the food is really great. I mean, like *they* know what's good for us to eat, don't they? And, like, we can eat whatever we want at home, can't we?"

She paused to pore over her notes and chew her gum.

"Well, so, like, I guess that's about it for that point." She clicked her heels all the way to her seat, then looked around the room to see if anyone was noticing.

Earnest swallowed twice, then three times. His heart was racing again, but not as bad as before. He forced himself to walk slowly to the podium, where he spread out his notes with shaking hands.

Earnest brushed the hair from his eyes and began talking very softly. Then he remembered to speak up. Now he was in full swing.

"So," he went on, "I think we could have tastier

meals and still be plenty healthy. As you know, we have spinach every Monday and beets on Wednesday and fish sticks on Friday. Half the kids don't eat these things. They just get thrown away. How can we be healthy if we don't eat the healthy stuff?"

Earnest pulled a paperback book from his rear pocket and thumbed through it. Then he went on. "Why don't we ever have things like pizza or tacos? Or strawberry shortcake?" He stopped thumbing through the book. "Okay, here's what I was looking for. Now, did you know that strawberries have more iron and fiber and phosphorus than spinach? And three times as much vitamin C?" He stopped to look around the room and see who was listening. "And also," he added, "Spinach has a lot of sodium, and that's not good for people."

He flipped over a few pages. "And here's something else. A large slice of pizza has 180 calories, but five of those greasy fish stinks—I mean *sticks* —have 500 calories. Calories make you fat."

He studied the book again. "And another thing. Pizza has thirteen times as much calcium as fish sticks, plus more iron and lots of vitamin A."

Shirley Bratley yawned a long, long yawn, then

put her head down on her disk and began to snore,
just softly enough that the teacher could not hear
her.

The class began to giggle at her, and Mrs. Black
said, "I hear some giggling. That tells me somebody is not paying attention."

Earnest glared at Shirley for a long time. His
face was red, and he started to say something to
her, but didn't. He took a deep breath.

"Well, I guess that's all I want to say on that
point." He took another deep breath and hurried
back to his seat.

One brainy boy on the front row applauded,
but no one joined him.

Meanwhile, the debate in Sonny's sixth grade
class was just getting started.

Mr. Watts laid down the rules of the debate,
then motioned to Jonah Yoder to begin.

Jonah stood up to his full height and swaggered
up to the teacher's podium. In his hands was a
tattered old softball, which he juggled back and
forth from one hand to the other.

Mr. Watts pointed to a large plastic trash can in
the corner of the room. "Jonah, let's put the softball in the can with the other sports equipment,
please."

Jonah tossed his head back to flip the mop of hair out of his eyes. "I need this ball to calm my nerves," he replied with a grin. It was plain to see Jonah was not nervous at all.

Mr. Watts rolled his eyes. "All right. Keep the ball, but let's get on with the debate, okay?"

Jonah looked pleased with himself. He gazed around the room with a glowing face. One of his friends whispered, "Go, Odor, go!"

Jonah juggled the ball some more, searching for his opening words. Then, in a loud, silly voice he said, "Well. I guess you might call me old fashioned. All us Amish guys are. We ain't into a lotta fancy stuff, see? We go for the plain stuff."

He waved his hand toward the ceiling lights. "This here school is what we call fancy. Yep. You got 'lectric lights and running water ... and a furnace. All that fancy stuff." He paused to let his words sink in, than added, "What do we need a new school for when this one has more stuff than I got at my own house?"

The class was smiling and chuckling to themselves.

Mr. Watts waved his hands. "Quiet, please. Jonah, you have used the word 'stuff' four times now."

Sonny was listening to all this from his window seat, leaning his chin on his hand. In his eyes was a look of admiration for Jonah.

Jonah began again. "At my house we don't even have rest rooms," he pointed out, "unless you call a hole in the ground a rest room." He laughed at his own joke.

"When we moved into the house it had all those 'lectric wires and stuff, so's we unscrewed all the bulbs and just let the 'lectricity run out onto the floor. That took care of that."

Again the class laughed. Mr. Watts quieted them, then added, "Jonah, try to stick to the topic of the debate."

Jonah nodded. He held up his old softball and said, "You know, a new school will cost a lotta money. I say, why don't we take all that money and buy something good, like new softballs . . ."

"How 'bout a room deodorizer," one boy on the front row quipped. He was too close to Jonah not to notice the barnyard smell.

Fifteen minutes later Jonah was still talking and enjoying it. Sonny shifted in his seat. He rolled up his sleeves because the room was getting warm. Above him one of the lights was flickering and humming, and it seemed to hypnotize Sonny, the boy next to him was slowly drumming his pencil on his desk, over and over again.

Sonny slumped in his seat, then laid his head on his on his desk. He began to breathe slower and slower.

At last Jonah was finished. He swaggered to his seat.

The teacher stepped to the front of the room. "Thanks, Odor. I mean, Jonah." He looked toward the window. "And now, we will hear from Sonny Wheeler."

The class whirled around to see what Sonny would do, but Sonny was sound asleep. Mr. Watts shook his head and pointed to another nearby student. "Albert, you want to punch Sonny so we can go on with this? It seems our presidential hopeful is in deep meditation."

Albert smacked Sonny on the shoulder so hard that Sonny woke up with fire in his eyes. He clomped up front, rubbing his shoulder and looking irritated.

Sonny's speech was much shorter than Jonah's. He concluded by saying, "So, I think a new school would make us all feel better." He paused and grinned at Jonah. "And it would smell a lot better, too."

When the noon bell sounded, Earnest sped from his classroom to his locker. He wriggled out his box of chocolates and galloped away to the sixth grade doorway. When the kids began coming out, he was standing there munching on a chocolate and holding the box so everyone could see it.

"Hi, Earnest, whatcha got?" one blonde girl chirped. She started to reach for a chocolate, but Earnest pulled the box away.

"Come on, share!" she complained.

"Glad to," Earnest replied. "*If* you promise to vote for my brother Sonny."

In a few minutes the box was empty.

7 • Surprises

Very early Friday morning Sonny crawled out of bed, dressed, and headed for the garage. It was still dark when he flipped on the garage light and set to work on his special project.

At breakfast he bounded into the kitchen, his face aglow.

"What are you so chipper about?" his mother asked. "What are you doing out there anyway?"

"Yeah," Earnest added. "What's the big secret? What are you doing with all those bed sheets? Making bandages for all the losers?"

Sonny crammed Wheaties into his mouth and mumbled, "You'll see soon enough. Today at noon, to be exact. It's gonna be *big*, I can tell you that." He wiped his mouth with his T-shirt. "I'm gonna put the name Earnest Wheeler on the map. Oh, by the way, Dad, you got any kind o' heavy cord? You know, like strong fishing line, or somethin'?"

Mr. Wheeler leaned back in his chair and stretched, just thinking for a few moments. Then he sat back down. "You know that big junk drawer under the basement workbench? There's a roll of nylon string in there that I bought to make a trotline, then never got around to it. It's pretty heavy stuff. You could tow a car with it, I 'spect."

"Perfect!" Sonny sang out. He leaped up and headed for the basement.

The boys could hear the first bell ringing across the ball diamond as they drew near the old building.

At morning recess, Earnest was taking a poll in the hallway. On the wall behind him was a poster-board sign that said, "Presidential Poll. Your opinions welcome." A line was forming at the sign. Earnest set up a card table with a chair for himself. On the table he set out some of his posters about Sonny and a dish of gumdrops with a little card on the dish that said, "Free."

As the first boy prepared to give his opinion, Earnest licked his thumb and opened his notebook. Shawn, the first "customer," was munching gumdrops and looking eager.

"Okay, Shawn," Earnest said, "How do you feel about Sonny Wheeler for president, on a scale of one to five. 'One' means you definitely plan to vote for him, and 'five' means you are definitely going to vote against him."

Shawn grabbed another fistful of candy. "Oh, I don't know," he said with a chewing sound. "Maybe a two. No, make that a three." He started to reach for more candy, but Earnest clamped his hand over the dish. "This candy is for 'ones.' Please move along. Thank you."

In a few minutes the line began to thin out. Earnest felt someone tugging at his sleeve from behind. He turned around to find Cherry standing there looking somber.

"Earnest, I need to talk to you. Right now."

Earnest paused, then closed his notebook. "Sorry, guys, the polls are closed." He dumped the remaining candy into his jacket pocket.

Cherry pulled Earnest into an empty classroom

and shut the door. Out of her pocket she fished a crumpled piece of paper and flattened it out. "I got some information for you," she whispered.

Earnest eyes grew large. "All right! Whatcha got?"

Cherry put the paper behind her back and held out her hand. "Where's the chocolates? You promised me two chocolates for each piece of information."

Earnest pranced impatiently. "You'll get your chocolates. Just give me the stuff, will ya?"

"Okay. I've got four things. That's eight chocolates you owe me."

Earnest rolled his eyes. "C'mon, will ya? The bell's gonna ring."

"Okay. First of all, I heard Sugar Brat say to her best friend—she said, 'I don't really care if I win the election or not, I just want to see Earnest lose.'"

"She said that? What a pig! And she tries to look so sweet."

"*And*, I caught her writing bad things about you on the wall in the girls restroom."

"Bad things?"

"Dirty words and stuff."

"I'm gonna tell the principal."

"Too late, I erased everything after she left."

"Okay, that's two things. Then what?"

"Well, you aren't gonna like this next one. She's been telling all her friends to call you Ernie, 'cause she knows how much you hate that."

Earnest turned a bright red in the face. "She *what?* That's going too far. She's gonna pay for this, believe me."

Cherry looked puzzled. "But you call *her* 'Sugar Brat.'"

"That's different. She doesn't mind being called that."

"Oh." Cherry looked at her notes. "And the other thing is, she's giving money to kids who promise to vote for her. Her dad gives it to her."

"What? That's bribery!" Earnest roared.

"That's the word I was trying to think of," Cherry said. "The other day, when you promised to give me chocolates."

Earnest's eyes shifted nervously. "That's different. I'm giving you candy because you *work* for me. She's just . . . she's just trying to buy friends."

"Oh."

"Hey, thanks, Cherry," Earnest said, when he heard the bell. "Keep your ears open. And don't worry about the chocolates. You'll get 'em."

Meanwhile, in the sixth-grade room, Sonny was fidgeting at his desk during silent reading time. He kept glancing at the clock. All at once he sprang up and tromped straight to the teacher's desk. He stood there waiting for Mr. Watts to put down his grading pencil.

"Yes?" Mr. Watts said, looking up.

"Can I go now?" Sonny begged. "Remember? What I talked to you about?"

Mr. Watts looked at his watch. "Oh, yes, I almost forgot. It's time, isn't it? Sure, Go on. And good luck!"

When Sonny had been gone a couple minutes, Mr. Watts stood up and motioned for attention. "I would like to make an announcement. At the noon hour there is going to be a special election event out by the ball diamond. The fifth and sixth grades are both urged not to miss this event."

The kids looked at each other with puzzled eyes.

Sonny, meanwhile, was leaping the fence to his own yard. He went straight to the garage and heaved the door upward. The sunlight shined on the garage floor. There lay a huge white kite, almost as big as the floor itself. It was bigger than the car that usually filled the space. A large diamond-shaped frame of cane poles was covered with white bed sheets that Sonny had carefully sewn to the edges. On the front of the kite, in big red letters, were painted the words, "VOTE FOR EARNEST."

Sonny was smiling as he dragged the kite out of the garage and tested its string. He glanced at the treetops to see if the wind was still blowing. The trees waved their branches slowly back and forth, up and down, as if to say, "Go for launch."

Sonny wrestled the monster flyer over the fence and onto the ball diamond. The big kite jerked back and forth in his hands, like some kind of living creature trying to escape. It was all he could do to hold it still.

Out of the corner of his eye he could see his friends and classmates lined up against the school building, looking his direction. Others were pressed against the windows, straining to see.

Sonny waited for a pause in the breeze, then tipped the monster up on end and unrolled some line from his string stick. the kite just sat there like a big billboard, wobbling slowly back and forth.

Sonny was not ready when the next breeze arrived. Suddenly the heavy line began to whirr through his hand. "Ouch!"he yelled, when the nylon line burned his palms.

The kite moved swiftly away from him like a frightened animal. Sonny gasped and clutched the stick with both hands. The kite bounced along the grass pogo-like for several yards, then suddenly leaped into the air like a science-fiction helicopter.

"Whoooooooooo!" Sonny screamed. The stick full of string whirred in his hand like it was motorized. Then the kite jerked the stick from his hands and dragged it along the ground like a rabbit fleeing from a dog.

Sonny wasted no time getting to it, but he was falling behind. He glanced up and saw that the kite was high in the air and growing smaller fast. It was headed toward the school.

Sonny stretched his legs as far and as fast as he could run, but the stick was hopping away from him. Then, all of a sudden, the stick caught in some weeds. The kite line went taut, and the kite stood still just long enough for Sonny to dive on the string.

The stick was almost empty now, so Sonny wrapped the line around his right wrist and forearm. Once, twice, three times.

There was no warning for what happened next. The gently noontime breeze turned into a powerful jet-like stream of air. The big, strong kite wrenched at Sonny's right arm like and evil monster. Sonny's feet began to leave the ground! For several seconds he sailed along through the air, with his feet only touching the grass now and then. He clawed at the grass with his feet, but it was useless. He tried to lay all his weight into the string, but he only landed long enough to bounce back into the air.

The next time he looked up, he saw the windows of the first grade classroom coming at him. "Ohhhhhh," he moaned, and he braced himself for the crash.

Just the the wind shifted. the heavy kite paused in it flight, then turned and dived straight for the school. The line went slack, and Sonny tumbled to the ground and rolled into the side of the building.

"Ohhhhhh," he moaned over and over, rubbing his sore feet and his swollen forearm. In the distance he could see some of his friends coming towards him at a run. He lay there breathing hard, then rolled over and glanced up. He could see his kite tangled in the top of the fire escape. The sticks were broken and the sheets torn. Only the name "Earnest" was still readable.

"Ohhhhhh," he moaned again. "All that work for nothing. Ohhhhhh."

8 • Checking the Score

Some of the guys were playing softball on roller skates when Sonny danced out of the cafeteria. The infielders were rolling back and forth on the asphalt, shouting to Jonah Yoder, who was at bat.

The first pitch was high. Jonah merely reached up, caught it in his left hand, and flicked it back to the pitcher. The next pitch was better, and Jonah calmly smashed it with an explosive sound. The ball shot into center field like a mortar shell from a big gun. Jonah skated backwards around the bases, enjoying the cheers of his friends.

The game was over. Jonah skated over to where Sonny was sitting next to the building.

"Hey Wheeler!" a redheaded boy hollered. "Nice show with the kite!"

"Yeah," another boy added. "great promo."

Jonah sprawled out by his lunch box and opened it. He pulled out a can root of beer, opened it and used his ball glove like a big hand to hold the can. Then he lifted out a tiny television and tuned in the noon news. With a paperback in one hand and a roast beef sandwich in the other, he began his meal.

Sonny watched all this in silence. "You know, Odor," he said at last. "You smell like a cow that just ran the Boston Marathon."

Jonah just smiled and went on chewing his sandwich.

"Do you really want to be President of the United States?" Sonny asked.

Jonah nodded.

"But I thought you Amish guys quit school after the eighth grade and never get involved in politics."

Jonah nodded again. "But I ain't gonna do it. I wanna learn everything I can. My dad says I'm 'chairminded.'"

What's that?"

"You know. I like to read. I sit in a *chair* and read."

Sonny grinned. "Listen, Odor, I want you to know that no matter who wins this election . . . well, I think you're a great guy." He paused a moment, then added, "I would be honored to be your vice president."

Jonah chomped away on a raw potato and smiled. "That's good," he mumbled, "cause I'm gonna *win*."

When the last bell of the day rang, Sonny ambled down to Earnest's room to shake some hands and urge his friends to vote for his brother.

Cherry joined the two of them as they strolled home. "I've got some more information," Cherry announced, pulling a piece of notebook paper from one of her books.

Earnest studied the paper and frowned.

"When do I get my chocolates?"

"You'll get 'em soon enough."

Cherry broke away and headed for her own house.

On Saturday the boys slept in till noon. In the afternoon they worked on banners and buttons for the convention that would be held on Monday.

At Sunday dinner Sonny was bragging about his speech.

His father listened with an amused look on his face. "How did your debate go, Sonny?"

Earnest began to laugh. "It went fine after he woke up."

Sonny glared at his brother. "How did you know about that?"

Earnest calmly shrugged. "I have *sources*."

Sonny took a long drink of chocolate milk and belched. "You know," he said, "We have this election sewed up. We could quit today and win it."

Earnest nodded. "Oh, by the way, here's a list of names from my poll. These kids said they were definitely voting for you."

Sonny grabbed the list and scanned it. "What? Jilbert Ganz is voting for me? I thought she hated my guts. And Karen Bland? I thought she was Jonah Yoder's good friend. I guess you never know." He folded up the list and stuffed it in his back pocket. "Thanks. I can use these names to get my parade organized. I'm gonna pull off a big parade, all the way from downtown. Earnest, you'll be world famous when I'm through with you."

Earnest peered suspiciously from under his dark

brow. "I just hope your parade doesn't crash into the fire escape. Me, I'm gonna do a telephone blitz tonight. *Your* name will be a household word when I'm done. Pass the beans, please."

"A household word?" Mr. Wheeler asked. "You mean like Drano or Tidy Bowl?"

"Oh, Dad."

Mr. Wheeler chuckled at his own wit and wiped steak grease from his lips. "Have you guys ever heard of 'overkill?'" he asked.

Sonny and Earnest looked at hach other blankly. "What's overkill?"

"Well, you know that orange juice commercial on TV? The one you loved when it first came out?"

"Yug," Earnest moaned. "If I see that commercial one more time I will *spit*."

"That's just what I mean," their father went on. "It's possible to try too hard, you know? People can get tired of hearing your name and decide to vote against you just because they're bored."

Earnest sneered. "No way, Dad. I mean, who's gonna vote for Sugar Brat? Except for her three friends. What a snot! Do you know she's going around school telling everyone to call me Ernie? I could *kill* for less than that."

"Don't say that, Earnest," his mother warned. "Not even in fun." She passed the rolls around and added, "You know, my mother used to say that there's bad in the best people and there's good in the worst people."

"Well, Grandma never met Sugar Brat."

"You mean there's nothing at all good about her?"

Earnest gave a thumbs down sign. "Zip, zero, zilch!"

Sonny belched again. "Oh, she has pretty hair. And a nice voice."

Earnest scowled. "So does a wolf."

Mrs. Wheeler added, "I thought you said she got the second best grades in class, Earnest."

Earnest picked up his steak knife and rubbed his thumb against the sharp edge. "Well," he said in a serious voice, "It doesn't matter, 'cause I'm going to get *revenge*." He slashed the knife through the air and gritted his teeth.

Mr. Wheeler calmly reached over the table and squeezed Earnest on the wrist with his massive hand, and the knife dropped to the table. "*Love* is the best revenge," he said, softly but firmly.

"What's that supposed to mean?" Earnest growled.

"Just what I said. If you really want to get even with someone, do it with love. It burns them up. People can fight hate, but they don't know how to fight love."

Earnest looked at his father with one eyebrow cocked, as if to say, "Poor Dad. He's living in a dream world."

Earnest stood up. "*Winning* is the best revenge," he said in a loud voice. He pulled a piece of paper from his back pocket and waved it around. "See this? This is my acceptance speech. That's how sure I am."

Mrs. Wheeler reached up and straightened his collar in back and brushed some bread crumbs from his shirtsleeve. "Well, boys, democracy is a funny thing. You can never tell who's going to win until the votes are counted."

Earnest jerked away from her and tromped to his room. He slumped in his desk chair and scowled at his computer for several minutes, just thinking. Then he printed out a list of names and phone numbers for his calling campaign.

When he had calmed down, he reached for a small pad of pink paper and a yellow pencil. For a while he just doodled on the paper, then he printed his father's words, "Love is the best revenge."

He stared at the words a few minutes, then tore off the sheet and wadded it up. He aimed the paper ball at the wastebasket, but at the last moment he stopped. He pried open the paper and smoothed it out on the desk and read it one more time.

"Love is the best revenge," he said softly to himself. Slowly he scratched his chin. "Hmmm . . ."

9 • The Convention

When Sonny awoke Monday morning he was in his old car, buried under seven blankets. He sat up, stretched, and peeled an election poster off the window so he could see outside. He could see light in the kitchen, so he wrapped a blanket around himself and traipsed up the porch steps and into the house.

A few minutes later he emerged with his brother. Each of them was toting a large cardboard box full of posters, banners, and buttons for the convention. Sonny's boom box sat on top of his

things. In a few minutes they arrived at school and went to their classrooms.

"Pardon me, please, coming through," Earnest said, squeezing into the doorway of his classroom. He sat his box down and dusted his hands off. When he looked up, Shirley Bratley was grinning at him. Her friends were gathered around her, all of them grinning an evil grin.

"Hi, *Ernie*," they said in unison.

Earnest blushed and gritted his teeth. Then, slowly, he seemed to relax. Softly he said, "Hi, girls. Hi, Shirley. You look very nice today."

"What's wrong with you, Wheeler? You always call me Sugar Brat."

Earnest shrugged. "Well, I decided that isn't a very good name for a nice girl who might be the next president."

Shirley looked at her friends with a twisted face. "Eeyew, you are strange, *Ernie*. Let's get outta here, girls, before we catch the strangies."

Earnest smiled and took his seat.

Mrs. Black waved her hand for order. She was smiling a full, clean smile. "All right, let's calm down. We have a lot work to do here this morning so we can have our convention in the afternoon."

The morning seemed to drag along, and Earnest

checked his watch at least a hundred times. Finally the lunch bell rang, and the crowd followed the hamburger smell to the cafeteria.

Earnest was the first one back from lunch. He found Mrs. Black already setting up two large tables, one for the Democrats and one for the Republicans. Earnest helped her cover the tables with white paper, then trimmed them with red and blue crepe paper streamers.

As the other kids arrived, Mrs. Black showed Earnest how to inflate the red balloons with a small tank of helium gas. She left him in charge.

"Trying to be the teacher's pet, *Ernie*?" Shirley said, with a sneer.

Earnest locked eyes with her, his face stern. Then he softened into a smile. "Here," he said. "Would you like to be in charge of this? I can do something else."

"Eeyew," Shirley said. "There he goes again, girls. Stay away from weird Ernie, or you will get weird all over you."

Mrs. Black put on a tape of patriotic music, and the room filled with the strains of *America the Beautiful*. Balloons were dancing and bobbing around the room, and some of the kids were swatting them with rulers and notebooks.

Earnest taped a long "VOTE FOR EARNEST" banner to the front of the Republican table, then laid out some buttons he had made from poster-board and safety pins. On each one he had stuck a paper seal of an elephant and added the words. "Elect Earnest."

Mrs. Black filled a punch bowl with red punch, and another larger bowl with pretzels of all shapes and sizes. The kids crunched them greedily and washed them down with the red liquid.

At one-thirty, Mrs. Black blew a whistle for attention.

"Okay, let's get in our seats and quiet down."

When everyone was ready, Mrs. Black talked to the class about democracy and elections. Then she pointed to a sturdy box in the corner of the room and said, "When you come in tomorrow, we will ask you to check your ballot." She held one up for them to see. "Then fold it and drop it into the box." She paused and looked at Shirley Bratley. "And now, we are ready for a short speech from the Democratic candidate."

Shirley swaggered and clicked her way to the front. She turned around, leaned on the teacher's desk and smiled sweetly at the class. She blew her bangs from her eyes and said, "Wellll, I just want to say, like, thanks to all my friends who, like, helped me beat . . . er, I mean who helped me, you know, like with all the work and everything. I will be proud to serve as president. I think I can do a better job than *some* people—I mean, like *Ernie* Wheeler. Like, who wouldn't?" She cackled like a witch, then added. "Beating him will be, like, more fun than being president, you know?" She smacked her gum, trying to think of something else to say, then clicked back to her seat to a round of applause.

Mrs. Black nodded. "Thank you, Shirley. And, Earnest?"

Earnest stepped briskly to the front of the room. He stuffed his hands deep in his pockets and cleared his throat.

"I, uh . . . I also want to thank all my friends and Mrs. Black for letting us hold the election. I would like to be your president a lot, and uh, to get some changes in the cafeteria." He shifted his feet and scratched his eyebrow with his thumb, then looked toward Shirley.

"But if I'm not elected, I think my opponent will do a good job too. She's a very smart person . . . and I would be proud to work for her." He shifted his feet again.

"And, well, I guess that's about it."

There was clapping as he took his seat, and Shirley stared at him with a strange expression on her face, as if she didn't know what to think of him.

Meanwhile, two blocks from school, Sonny was putting together his parade.

"Okay, you guys!" he was shouting. "Everybody got a boom box? We have one extra here if we need it." Everyone nodded. "All right. Tune your box to 105, the big band station." Dials spun as the thirteen kids tuned to a station that broadcast march music.

Sonny was clutching a big, homemade flag that said, "Vote for Earnest." Behind him stood a girl holding a large stuffed animal—a pink elephant with one ear missing and purple nail polish on its toes.

At last all the radios were tuned to 105. It sounded like one radio playing from many different speakers.

Sonny waved his flag and shouted, "Okay, let's go!"

All the radios went up to full volume as the parade started moving. It sounded like a full-size band coming down the street. Each girl and boy

was wearing something red as a uniform. They wore red baseball caps, red sweaters, and red tennis shoes.

Cars began to slow down and people stopped and pointed as the parade left the downtown and neared the school.

In a few minutes Sonny marched the troupe right up to the fifth-grade window. There the kids stood, marching in place to the sound of the music.

In seconds, a dozen faces appeared in the windows. Earnest's face showed with a look of shock, then vanished. Finally, Mrs. Black's face came into view, and she motioned to her class to open two of the windows. For several moments they all listened to the music.

All of a sudden the music stopped and a commercial came on.

Hold it, the announcer said in a booming voice that echoed across the schoolyard. *Did you forget to do something before you left the bathroom this morning? Better go back and do it.*

The parade burst into violent laughter.

Don't start your day, the radios boomed, *without Mellowsmooth, the fiber laxative that will make you as regular as the sunrise. Available at your druggist or discount store.*

Mrs. Black turned red in the face and quickly shut the windows.

The laughter continued even after the music returned, but Sonny lost no time leading the parade on into the building and down the hall to the sixth grade room.

As he turned the parade into his classroom, he could see other classes peering through their doorways to see what the music was all about. Then he saw the principal running towards him, and he ducked into the room.

Seconds later Mr. Watts dashed out the door to calm down the principal.

The class cheered as Sonny's parade members stacked their boom boxes by the door and took their seats.

When Mr. Watts returned, a pink, one-eared elephant was sitting on his desk.

10 • The Winners

"My convention was a drag," Sonny said to his brother on the way to school Tuesday, election day. "After the parade, it was all downhill. Mr. Watts played this real dorky music—almost put us to sleep. Then he told us a bunch o' boring stories about elections he remembered back in the sixties. For refreshments he served us these cookies that looked and tasted like baked sand—I think he musta made 'em himself. Then we spent the rest of the afternoon playing a bunch of dumb games."

Cherry joined the two of them as they neared

the school. "Hey, you guys!" she called out. "I hope you both win." She ran ahead of them, then turned and blocked Earnest's path. Earnest almost tripped over her.

She stood with her hands on her hips looking stern. "Where's my chocolates?" she demanded. She held out her hands. "I want them *now*."

She was trying to sound fierce, but her hand looked like a doll's hand and her voice had voice had all the terror of a mouse.

Earnest grinned, then slung down his book bag and opened it. "Here. All of them. They're yours. You earned 'em." He shoved the box at her. "There's twenty-four in there. Try not to get sick."

Cherry's face turned a happy pink. She whirled around and took off running for class, all the while clutching the box to her bosom. "Thanks!" she hollered over her shoulder. Already she had a chocolate in her mouth.

Before Sonny left Earnest to go to his room, he stopped and held up his palm. "Here's to the winners," he said. His brother slapped his hand and grinned. "Easy win," he said.

When Earnest ambled into class, several kids were standing by the voting booth Mrs. Black had made by hanging a bed sheet across one corner of

the room. She handed Earnest an official ballot—
a small square of paper with his name and Shirley's name typed neatly in the middle.

"Just circle the name of the person you want to
vote for," she explained.

"Can I vote for myself?" Earnest asked.

"Of course! Who else would you vote for? You
do want to win, don't you?"

Earnest took his turn in the booth. He closed the
sheet behind him and looked around. On a small
flower stand Mrs. Black had arranged a desk lamp
and a coffee cup with pencils in it. Above the
stand was an American flag stuck to the wall.

Earnest pulled a yellow pencil from the cup and
circled his name with a flourish of the pencil and
started to fold it up. Then he stopped and opened
it back up. Slowly he erased the line around his
name, then circled Shirley's name. He folded the
slip, left the booth and dropped the paper in the
slot on top of the big box.

At noon, another teacher came to class to help
Mrs. Black count the ballots. Three times they
counted them, just to be sure. Then Mrs. Black
wrote a name on a card and sealed it in an envelope. Several kids tried to peek over her shoulder,
but she shooed them away with a mean look.

The afternoon seemed to last forever. Earnest chewed all the erasers off his pencils, then bit his fingernails until they were bleeding. His eyes didn't seem to focus on his book very well, and he found himself staring out the window every two or three minutes. Every now and then Shirley Bratley turned around and stared at him with a curious look. Earnest returned each look with a smile and a wave.

When Earnest thought he would die of suspense, Mrs. Black finally reached in her desk drawer and pulled out the envelope.

"All right, class. Silent reading time is over. I want you to clear your desks for the day."

There was a flurry of papers and books, then everything grew very quiet.

Once again Mrs. Black spoke to them about elections, and Earnest shifted in his seat impatiently. Then she reviewed the past week for them.

At last she raised her voice and said, "Now I know you are all anxious to know who will be President of the United States for one day." Carefully she tore off the end of the envelope and blew into it. The card came sliding out and dropped to the floor. Quickly she rescued it and held it to her bosom so no one could see the name.

"Just to show you how important it is for every-one to vote, I want to point out that this election was very, very close. The winner got only *one* vote more than the loser. Just *one* vote."

The class gasped and groaned.

Earnest swallowed hard. He played with his collar, stretching it open wider and wider, until the button popped off and rolled down the aisle.

Meanwhile, Shirley Bratley seemed to be frozen in her seat. She was sitting straight and tall with her arms tucked neatly at her side. On her face was a nervous, silly smile.

Mrs. Black looked around the room, then at Earnest. Then she looked at Shirley, and finally at her card.

Earnest clutched his stomach, feeling like he was going to throw up. His eyes swam in and out of focus until he had to close them.

Mrs. Black took a deep breath. "The next President of the United States is . . . Miss Shirley Bratley."

There was a moment of silence, then the class screamed and applauded, loud and long. Some of Shirley's friends crowded her desk and hugged her, but she was still sitting straight and unmoving as if in a trance.

Earnest tried to clap, but his hands seemed like concrete blocks, and he couldn't quite get them together for some time.

Shirley stood up and looked around on the clapping students. She took a bow, but she didn't seem as cocky as she did before the vote. Then she looked straight at Earnest.

Suddenly Earnest seemed to come alive. He rose to his feet and clapped as hard as he could clap. Shirley's mouth fell open when she saw him. Soon everybody was standing with Earnest and clapping and whistling.

When the applause finally died down, Shirley gave a very short acceptance speech, after first removing the gum from her mouth.

The final bell rang, and Earnest was the first one out the door, leaving his book bag on his seat in his haste. He was halfway down the hall when a small hand squeezed his arm and stopped him. He turned around. It was Shirley.

"Hey, Wheeler, thanks," she said meekly.

"For what?" Earnest replied.

"For being such a good loser," she said, looking at the floor. "Like, I'm not sure I deserved to win this, you know?"

Earnest was blinking rapidly to keep the tears

from spilling out. He shrugged and said, "I'm just glad it's only make believe." Then he added, "Just one thing. If you ever run for president, I mean, for *real*, you know?"

Shirley nodded.

"Well," he went on, "better plan on being *vice* president."

Shirley smiled. She wrapped one arm around him and gave him a nice hug, then she whirled around and headed back to her fans.

After school, Earnest was shuffling across the ball diamond with his head down when Sonny came up alongside him. He took one look at Sonny and said, "You too?"

Sonny nodded. "It was a *landslide*. I got *two* votes! Two votes out of twenty-one kids." He shook his head and chuckled to himself.

"You know," Sonny went on, "I've never seen Odor so happy. To tell the truth I'm glad he won. You know that softball he always carries with him no matter where he goes?"

Earnest nodded.

"Well, it's funny, but when he gave his acceptance speech, he actually put it down on the desk. Guess he doesn't need it any more. He looked almost naked without it. What a guy! You know, maybe he will be President some day. Can you see it? 'Ladies and gentlemen, the President of the United States, and Mrs. Odor!'"

At supper the boys were quiet, their minds sorting through the events of the past week.

After dessert Earnest pulled his acceptance speech from his pocket and looked at it longingly. Then he crumpled it up and shot it into the wastebasket.

The phone rang and Mrs. Wheeler answered it.

"Yes? Who? Cherry? Oh, nooo. Oh, the poor thing. Uh-huh. Yes, I'll tell them. And thanks so much for calling."

"Who was that?"

"Cherry's grandmother. Cherry was just taken to the emergency room about an hour ago."

"Cherry? What's wrong?" Earnest gasped.

"She overdosed."

"What?!" Sonny yelled. "Overdosed? Cherry doesn't do drugs."

Mrs. Wheeler smiled. "Not drugs ... chocolates. Twenty-four of them to be exact. Or so she told the doctors. She's gonna be all right." She looked at Earnest out of the corner of her eye. "I wonder where she got all those chocolates?"

Earnest shrugged. "Beats me."

Wheeler's Adventures

Wheeler's Big Break

Sonny and Earnest have a contest to see which one can fix the most broken items in one week.

Wheeler's Vacation

On a vacation to California, Earnest sets out to prove that he doesn't have to have fun if he doesn't want to.

Wheeler's Freedom

Sonny and Earnest are left home to take care of themselves for a whole week.

Wheeler's Campaign

The brothers agree to manage each other's campaigns for class president.